Home Sweet Home

Home Sweet Home

Jean Marzollo

ILLUSTRATED BY

Ashley Wolff

SCHOLASTIC INC.
New York Toronto London Auckland Sydney

ISBN 0-590-03490-1

Text copyright © 1997 by Jean Marzollo.
Illustrations copyright © 1997 by Ashley Wolff.
All rights reserved. Published by Scholastic Inc., 555 Broadway, New York, NY 10012,
by arrangement with HarperCollins Publishers.

12 11 10 9 8 7 6 5 4 3 2 1   8 9/9 0 1 2 3/0

Printed in the U.S.A   14

First Scholastic printing, January 1998

For Phoebe and Kirby
J. M.

For Jewell and Bud, with love
A.W.

Bless each bee

Each flower and tree

Each cloud in the sky

Each stalk of rye

Each fish, each bear

Each tender calf

Each tall giraffe

Bless each wren

Each rooster and hen

Each turtle and snake

Each duck and drake

Bless each ant

Each cactus plant

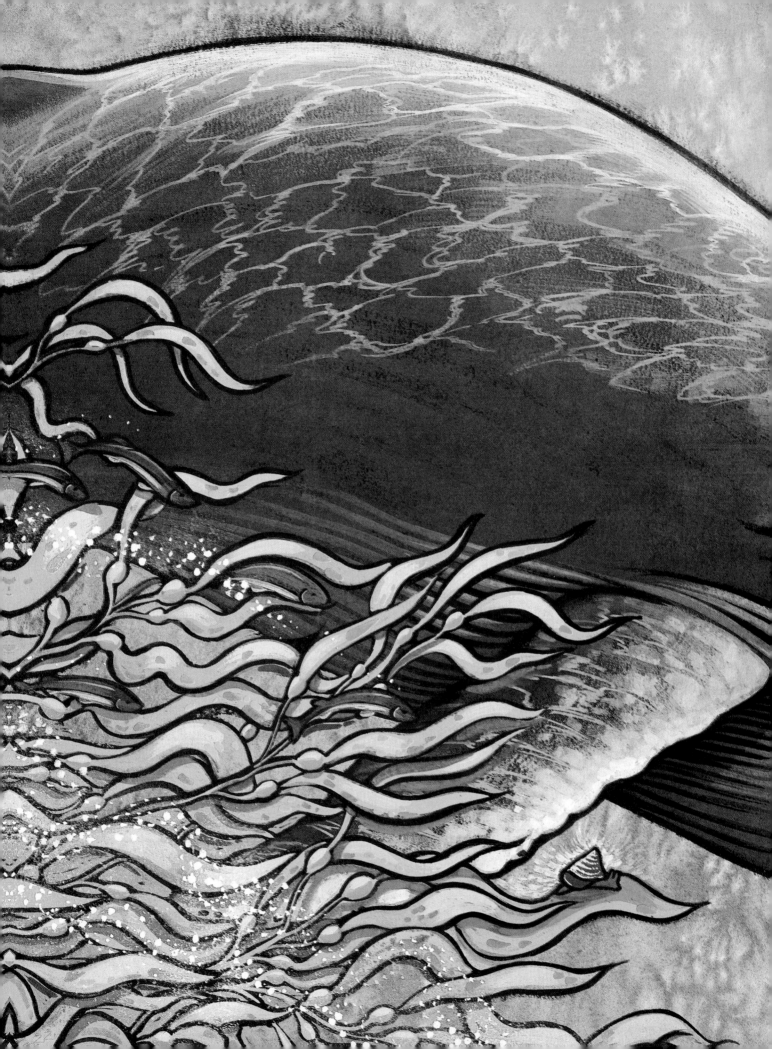

Each dolphin and whale

Each little snail

Bless each foal

Each tiny tadpole

Each apple and pear
Each breath of air

In our home called Earth.